Kid
CARAMEL
PRIVATE INVESTIGATOR

THE WEREWOLF OF PS 40

by Dwayne J. Ferguson

BOOKS

Just Us Books, Inc. • East Orange, New Jersey

Printed in Canada
12 11 10 9 8 7 6 5 4 3
Library of Congress Number Cataloging-in-Publication
data is available

ISBN: 0-940975-82-3 (paperback)

Cover illustration copyright 1998 by Don Tate
Interior design by DIEHARD Studio

He's Cool. He's a detective...
He's BACK!

Where or where has the werewolf gone?

Kid Caramel and his trusty sidekick, Earnie, are up against their biggest case yet: All the neighborhood pets are disappearing and no one has any idea what's going on. You can bet that Kid Caramel and Earnie are on the case. Things go fine until they start finding some very weird clues. Clues that point toward only one answer. And it's not a pretty one.

Well, Kid Caramel and Earnie are determined to get to the bottom of this new mystery. But there's just one small problem: The clues say there's a werewolf in town–and everyone knows werewolves aren't real–or are they?

Chapter One:
Back in the Classroom Again

It was the first day of school. Actually it was more of a parade of new clothes, notebooks, rulers, and sneakers, than the beginning of another great chapter in the lives of children everywhere. Everyone buzzed about, trying to impress each other, while butting their noses in everyone's business.

Sharktooth Williams, PS 40's bully supreme, only cared about one thing today: who the new teachers were. Through his underground network (kids he threatened to beat to a pulp) he'd discovered that there was indeed a new teacher, a Mr. Andrews, homeroom 109, Science.

Sharktooth shoved the kid next to him into a walk. Creepy Timmy was wiping something from his nose on his shirt. Sharktooth laughed. *No wonder they call him creepy,* he thought.

"C'mon Creepy, let's check this out."

They lumbered to the bulletin board in the first floor hall. Sharktooth checked the room assignments, and what do you know, he was assigned to Mr. Andrews's homeroom. Sharktooth grinned and headed off for class like a good student. Bribery and scare tactics were his best friends yet again. Today would be the day to reveal this year's 'new teacher prank'. A strange expression spread across his mug. It was a smile only a momma shark could love.

"I'll see ya at lunch, Creepy."

Creepy nodded and mumbled yes under his breath.

So preoccupied was Sharktooth with the news of the day, that he failed to notice his favorite scratching post, Earnest Todd, who snuck right by him.

Earnie wasn't exactly what you'd call the king of confidence, but he was the editor-in-chief of the school newspaper *The PS 40 Scoop*. That was more than enough clout to make Earnie somewhat popular in school. Not only was Earnie on the school newspaper, but he was best friends with the school's *numbero uno* up-and-coming super sleuth, Caramel Parks, a.k.a. Kid Caramel.

Earnie walked on his tippy toes, continuing to sneak past Sharktooth. He was unaware that at this particular moment in his life, Sharktooth couldn't care less about pounding on him. Earnie kept his eyes peeled for his life-long pal. He hadn't seen Caramel at all last week because Earnie was at summer camp.

Earnie was eager to show Caramel his new bookbag. It had a picture of an African-American Sherlock Homes and Watson silk screened on the back. It was one of the projects he had made while at camp. Of course Holmes was supposed to be Caramel, and his trusted sidekick Watson, was supposed to be himself.

Twenty minutes later, Earnie was ready to give up. *He'd meet Caramel in homeroom,* Earnie thought. Then a lightbulb went on in his head. "Of course, there's only two other places besides a crime scene and the arcade that Kid Caramel would be..."

The PS 40 library was as close to heaven on earth that Caramel thought he could get. Books to his left, books to his right. Somebody pinch him! The library was located on the top floor of the five story school. The seventh grade young adult section just received a new collection of *Captain Africa* and *Neate* novels and Caramel couldn't wait to dig in. The mystery books he'd read during the summer added fuel to the fires of his already over-active imagination. He walked to the front desk to check out his new treasures when Earnie ran in. He almost crashed right into his friend who was holding a mountain of books.

"Hey, Kid, welcome back to school!" Earnie said it with an eager smile that would make the Easter Bunny look mean by comparison.

Caramel's left eyebrow arched up.

"You've got to be kidding, Earn. 'Welcome back to school?' School's great and all, I hope you haven't been saying that all day. Have you?"

Earnie nodded his head.

Caramel punched him in the arm.

"Hey, never stop being you, buddy. Your strangeness is why you're my best friend."

They stopped at a long wooden table. Caramel separated the books, sliding seven of them to Earnie.

"I found those new UFO books you asked me to find for you. Enjoy."

"Thanks, Kid. Over the summer I decided that I'm gonna be an FBI agent. You know, like on the *X Files*." Earnie paused for a moment and sighed sadly.

"That is, if I don't get chewed up by you know who." Earnie frowned and took a folded piece of paper from his front pocket. He handed it to his friend.

Caramel read it aloud:

Dear little worm-head,

Me an' Creepy Timmy're gonna pound you into the pavement the first day of school. You might wanna wear somethin' you can get real dirty in. Hahahahah! From your bestest friends of all time, Sharktooth and Creepy. PS Tell your buddy Kid Marshmallow that he better go out and buy a suit of armor, cause I'mma open a can o' beat down on him too.

"This is great, Earn, not only are you going around the school greeting everyone with a big hearty welcome, we're being hunted by a shark in sneakers. And now he has a partner in crime."

"What are we gonna do, Kid?"

"Leave it to me, Earn. We just have to outsmart the old kingpin of slime at his own game," the boy genius said. "Let's check these books out and head down to homeroom."

Caramel placed his stack of books on the check-out counter. The librarian's eyes popped open. There were twenty-six books. Then she realized who was checking them out.

"All you can eat book buffet, I see,"

Ms. Oswald chuckled.

"Yes, ma'am," Caramel replied. "And I'd like to order a side of fries with these, please."

He and Ms. Oswald laughed. Earnie's eyebrows rose in surprise. Over the mountain of books, she saw the top of Earnie's head. "Hello, Earnest."

"Hello, Ms. Oswald", replied Earnie. "You can get French fries when you check books out now?" Earnie sounded so innocent, it made Caramel wince. "I'd like extra ketchup, please."

Another punch to the arm came from Caramel.

"It was just a joke, Earn. Next time the clue train passes this way, climb aboard."

Ms. Oswald shook her head, still laughing and whispered, "Kids," to herself. She began the laborious task of scanning the books' bar-codes.

"How was your summer, Caramel, Earnie?" She asked, pushing several gray strands of hair away from her face.

Caramel smiled and said, "I basically studied great mysteries on the internet. I love downloading files featuring great unsolved mysteries. You know, one day, I'm gonna solve a few, if not all of them!"

"Um, and me too, said his trusty side-kick,

Kid Earnie!" his best friend added with his chest out like a proud rooster.

"Kid Caramel and Kid Earnie...do you see a slight redundancy problem here, Earn?"

Earnie looked up at the taller boy. "Redun-who?"

"That means too much repetition. Too much of the same thing. In other words....change your nickname 'cause it's taken!"

They both laughed for a second until the librarian 'shushed' them into silence.

"Now you boys know better than to make all that racket in here," Ms. Oswald reminded them. She finished the huge task of scanning all of Caramel's books and slid the last of them towards the young detective.

"Thank you, ma'am. I can't wait to sink my eyes into these!"

Caramel's backpack was close to bursting, so he propped the remainder of his treasure under his arms.

"Well, we better get to class. Thanks a lot, Ms. Oswald," Caramel said, still trying to balance the books under his arms. As they headed out, Caramel stopped in his tracks. The books under his arms crashed to the floor.

"Earnie, look at this!"

Earnie dropped everything on the floor as well. He had no clue why, but since it seemed so urgent, he thought it the thing to do. Caramel held up the *Tanwood Times*. Earnie read the headline aloud.

> **Two dozen pets missing in Tanwood.**
> **Supermarkets missing meat.**
> **Is there a connection?**

"This has strangeness written all over it Earn'," Caramel said. He folded the paper and stormed out of the library.

Ms. Oswald caught up to Earnie before he could leave. "What's going on, Earnie?"

Earnie had a look of determination in his eyes.

"Looks like we've got a new case, Ms. Oswald," he said as he flashed his badge at her. He and Caramel had been awarded official Junior Detectives badges after their last caper.

Earnie left the library. And left Ms. Oswald with a pile of books on the floor.

Chapter Two:
The New Kid on the Block

The homeroom bell rang and suddenly Summer Vacation was officially OVER. The school maintenance crew had made improvements all over the building. Caramel and Earnie were sitting in relatively old chairs but the paint on the walls was new. There were even new lockers and gym equipment, thanks to donations from graduates who had gone on to college and had become successful in business. There were also some new lights and chalkboards. All this gave a "fresh start feeling" to the already modern class room.

But there was still the same old bully. Sharktooth had the most innocent look on his face that Caramel had ever seen. This meant he was up to no good. What else was new? Although he was sitting half way across the room from him, Caramel switched to his detective zoom vision (patent pending), and enlarged the area Sharktooth claimed as his own. As usual, Sharktooth's books and notepads were a mess, pages crumpled and torn. They sat on the floor next to his bookbag. The bookbag was such a disaster that it looked like you'd get what you deserved for opening it.

Caramel's eyes worked their way up and noticed the ever-present dirt on Sharktooth's sneakers and jeans. He thought to himself that the pants, at one time in the history of civilization, had been blue. Next was the sweater, which looked like it was used as a cape in a bull fighting competition. The bull probably lost. Caramel continued his scan and noticed something about Sharktooth that was so out of the ordinary that he had to do a double-take. Sharktooth's hands were actually clean!

Caramel leaned back in his chair, brainstorming. If Sharktooth's hands were clean, it meant that his practical joke for this year might involve something typically dirty or messy to handle; charcoal, paint or glue. Because, after he had used it, he'd have to wash it off. Caramel had to narrow it down to things one might find in a school; paint, glue, chalk. Caramel looked around the entire classroom. He made mental notes with his photographic mind. The windows weren't scratched, the desks weren't covered in graffiti, the teacher's desk wasn't covered with glue...then he looked at the chalkboard. It was shiny, as if it had recently been washed with a sponge. Even if the board had been washed at the beginning of the class, it would show signs of drying by now. At least ten minutes had passed since the homeroom bell rang. Caramel reasoned this was very interesting indeed.

Mr. Andrews walked to the center of the class.

"Good morning, class. I'm your new homeroom and Science teacher, Mr. Andrews. I'm looking forward to working with each of you this school year. If you have any questions or problems, be sure to ask."

The teacher opened the planner on his desktop and started roll-call. Halfway through, the door to the classroom opened and a new boy walked in. He had sandy brown hair, blue eyes, and freckles on one side of his face. Unlike the rest of the kids, who had on shorts, T-shirts and sneakers, he was dressed in a dress shirt, blazer and tie.

"Pardon, I'm sorry for ma' tardiness, sir. I'm Kayin McIntyre," he said with an accent that wasn't quite familiar to the class.

"Welcome Mister McIntyre. Please, find a seat and join the fun. In the future, be here on time."

"Thank ye', sir." Kayin weaved in between the occupied chairs until he found an empty spot. Right next to Sharktooth. Caramel, Earnie and most of the other students closed their eyes–and groaned.

Sharktooth leaned toward the newcomer, smelling fresh bait in his territory.

"So, what kinda stupid accent is that you got there, or is somethin' the matter with ya?" he asked with his fangs bared. There was a piece of meat stuck in between Sharktooth's teeth.

Kayin backed into his chair, disgusted and a bit confused. He had been told that the kids in America were different, but not this different.

"I-I'm from Scotland. My family and I moved here two months ago. By the by, what kind o' stupid accent is it that you've got there, boyo?"

Sharktooth's eyes popped wide open. What was this? A newbie trying to talk lip to the king of the hill?

"I hope ya kept yer plane receipt so you can get a refund for the return trip. Cause I'm sending ya home fer free right now!"

He made a massive fist and started the countdown to knock Kayin back to bonnie Scotland.

"I wouldn't advise that, Mister Williams," Mr. Andrews said sternly. "We're here to study from books, not with fists. Now sit down." Sharktooth sighed and looked up at the clock.

Caramel suddenly looked at Sharktooth's

bookbag again. A lightblub lit up in his head and he raised his hand.

"Earnie," he whispered, "I think I found a way to keep the shark at bay." Earnie smiled nervously, making sure Sharktooth wasn't paying attention to him. "I'll let you know when I'm ready to spring Operation Shark Hunt."

Mr. Andrews turned away from the boys and walked to the front of the room. He drew a picture of the moon on a flipchart. Then he drew a misty cloud around it.

"Did anyone notice the full moon last night?"

A girl name Maria raised her hand.

"Yes, it was real spooky like in the movies. My father put up garlic to protect our house from the bad spirits."

"Interesting," Mr. Andrews replied. "Like Maria's family, many people are believers in superstition. And many times these beliefs stem from nature's strange behaviors. For example, because our bodies are over 80% water, the full moon acts like a magnet on us just like it does on the ocean. Larger tidal waves occur on nights when the moon is full. So we scientists believe that some people act strangely because of the moon's

gravitational pull on us. It may explain th
werewolf superstition."

"I don't understand," said Ted from th
corner. He sat in the corner of all of his classes an
refused to sit anywhere else. Maybe the moon wa
full around Ted full-time.

Mr. Andrews explained. "In medieval times
there were many accounts of people who claime
they had changed into wolves. These occurrence
almost always happened during a full moon. An
the weird part about this is that these report
were recorded world-wide!"

Caramel raised his hand.

"I watched the news last night. They sai
since last month over twenty pets in Tanwoo
disappeared without a trace. Do you think that'
kind of strange?" He got out of his chair an
walked across the room.

"Young man, where do you think you'r
going?"

"Excuse me, Mr. Andrews," Caramel sai
politely. He walked over to an unsuspectin
Sharktooth and pulled him out of his seat an
towards the front of the classroom.

"On behalf of the class, my friend Sharktoot
and I would like to welcome you to PS 40. We'

ike to lead the class in the singing of our school song. Could everyone please stand?"

The class did so, unsure of what to make of the show. But they knew if Kid Caramel was calling Sharktooth his friend, something that would go down in history was about to happen. Some of them started giggling.

"Huh?" Sharktooth grunted in surprise. "I didn't even know we had a school song!" He yanked his arm from Caramel's grip but it was too late. He was already in front of the room.

"You'll have plenty of time practicing it in the Principal's office when I'm done with this," Caramel whispered. "There's only one way I can think of to prevent you and your goon from beating the pulp out of my best friend after school and this is it."

He winked at Sharktooth and smiled. Whether Caramel was scared of the bully, he couldn't tell.

"By the way, I forgot to buy that armor you mentioned in your letter. But you might need to purchase a pillow to rest your big head on during the year of detention you're about to get."

Mr. Andrews smiled and leaned against his desk.

"The school song just for me. I'm flattered.

Thank you, children. You may proceed when you're ready."

Before a single note was crooned, Caramel leaned back and 'accidentally' pushed Sharktooth against the chalkboard.

"Oops, sorry."

"Hey, you goof, the board's still wet with-"

"With what, Sharktooth?" Caramel asked as he walked to the bully's desk. He reached into Sharktooth's bookbag and pulled out a can of green paint.

"You wouldn't happen to recognize this, would you?"

His face filled with rage, Sharktooth tried to turn his head to see his paint-coated back.

"Sooner or later, I'm gonna knock your smile off, Parks!"

With that, he lumbered to his seat. He leaned back, forgetting about the wet paint on his shirt, and got stuck to the chair. He simply closed his eyes and growled.

Mr. Andrews stood in awe. "How on earth did you know he painted the chalkboard, Mister..."

"Parks, sir." Caramel answered. "When I came into the room, I noticed two strange things; one about Sharktooth himself, and one about his books. The first: Sharktooth's hands are never, I repeat, never clean. Not even on Thanksgiving. That alone told me he was up to something. And second, you reminded Sharktooth that we're here to study from books. Then it clicked. There was no reason for his books to be on the floor while his bookbag was still full. Which meant he carried his books in hands and had something fishy in the bag. Then I noticed that the chalkboard was wet, without any signs of drying for over fifteen minutes. That's about it, sir."

Mr. Andrews pointed a finger at the young man. "So, you must be the student I heard so much about. Let me guess, Kid Caramel."

Caramel, humble as always, simply nodded and smiled. He was taught never to brag, but to always use his intelligence to explain things when asked. He returned to his seat, setting his personal shields high enough to block the lasers from Sharktooth's eyes. Earnie gave him a 'thumbs up, despite the look he got from the school bully.

The school bell rang. Everyone grabbed their books and headed to first period. Before Caramel and Earnie could leave the room, they were herded like cattle into a corner by Sharktooth. He drooled under most circumstances but this time his mouth was in froth overdrive.

"You two are m-i-n-e! (Caramel was surprised Sharktooth could spell.) Do you get me? I mean you two are shark bait and like all good sharks, I'mma getcha when you least expect it. I'mma spring from the bottom of the ocean to chew you up...bones and all!"

Sharktooth pushed them both into the wall and stalked from the room like an alley cat having a bad fur day. Earnie was in shock and looked like a deer caught in oncoming headlights. Caramel just brushed off Sharktooth's threat and left the room. He called out, "Hey, Sharktooth!"

Every student within earshot stopped and turned.

Slowly, the super bully turned also. "What do ya want, wiener?"

Caramel smiled confidently, "You and me. Anytime...anywhere." He held his thumb up, then slowly rotated his wrist until the thumb pointed to the ground. With that, Kid Caramel turned and walked to his first class. Earnie tagged along closer than the boy detective's own shadow.

"Kid, you know your father doesn't want

you to get into fights," Earnie whispered, still a bit spooked out.

"I know, Earn, but sometimes you have to stand up to the bad guys. It lets them know that you're not afraid of them."

Caramel looked at his shorter friend. "You really ought to give it a try. You'll be like a dolphin. They're not afraid of sharks. Maybe then Sharktooth would leave you alone and find another person to bully."

"There's no way I could do that," said Earnie nervously. "Sharktooth's the single scariest monster I've ever known. He'd kick my face in just for fun. And then he'd hurt me."

"I never said you'd be able to beat him toe-to-toe," Caramel replied. "But he might respect you if he knew he couldn't scare you anymore. There are monsters everywhere, and we have to think we can beat them or we'll always be afraid of our own shadows."

At that moment, the school janitor, Earl Ritter, turned the corner, pushing a trash can on wheels. He was pushing the can as if he were in a tremendous hurry. He barely missed the boys. Earl lost control and crashed into the wall. The contents of the can flew across the hallway.

Caramel and Earnie started to help Earl with the mess when he held his hands up.

"Uh, that's all righty there, fellas. I can handle it from here, but thanks," he said with a slow drawl. Sounded like he was from down South. Way down South.

"Are you sure? It would be much faster if we helped," Caramel offered.

"No. No, I've got it just as fine as flyin', thanks again. Now you two just scoot on to class and let ol' Earl handle this here messy mess I made."

Kid Caramel studied the janitor like a bug under a microscope. His eye-spy camera took a quick snapshot, which the film lab in his brain began to develop immediately. Caramel processed the details.

Earl's forehead was washed in sweat like it was a hot summer day, but it was September and chilly. Earl had only been walking quickly, but not jogging or running. There was just too much sweat.

Earl Ritter was definitely nervous about something.

But what? Kid Caramel reached into his backpack and took out something he and Earnie had invented over the summer: the

"Caramel/Earnie Tracer," C.E.T. for short. It was nothing more than a walkie talkie taped to a micro-cassette player. They had painted it silver and written the initials C.E.T. in black marker.

Using his highly polished acting skills, Caramel pretended to slip on a piece of trash.

"Whoa!"

He fell to the floor right next to the garbage can. Earl was so busy trying to put everything back in that he hardly noticed the boy on the floor.

"I-I'm OK," Caramel reported, using the can to pick himself up. And, when he was almost fully standing, he dropped the C.E.T into the can. A glimmer of something sharp at the bottom of the trash can caught his eye. It was about two inches long and shaped like a small elephant tusk. He reached for it but Earl tapped him on the shoulder as his finger grazed it.

"I said I'll take it from here, boys. Now skidaddle!"

Caramel sighed in disappointment. A clue! A vital clue. He had to get it no matter what. But obviously not now. He nodded to Earnie and they walked away. Before they walked into Algebra class, Earnie took out the matching C.E.T. and turned it on.

They could hear Earl fussing to himself.

"All systems go," Earnie said.

"Check," Caramel replied. "I want to know the minute Earl leaves that trash can alone. There's a big-time clue in there."

"What do you think it is?" Earnie asked excitedly.

"A fang." Caramel started down the hall. "Well, we have to go to class now, but we can't just walk in there with our secret devices."

"OK, then, proceeding to Plan B."

Earnie unrolled a section of head phone cord and placed a listening piece into his ear. He tucked it down into his shirt and shaped the wire so it fit behind his ear. He plugged the cord into the C.E.T. and returned it to his bookbag.

"Total stealth mode activated," Earnie reported.

Caramel looked the hallway up and down. It was all clear. "Let's go in."

Chapter Three:
The Trouble with Fangs.

Algebra wasn't exactly Caramel's idea of a good time. Although he was good at it, he'd rather be solving brain-stumping mysteries. His mind was mostly on getting to the fang.

Earnie, on the other hand, was like a math magnet, and could easily figure out how many apples Bobby and Sue would have left before the 9:15 train met the 11:47 train in New Mexico during a thundershower.

Earnie studied the chalkboard. The problem stated: If Jane had three apples on her way to school and bumped into Tommy, who had two apples and 1 orange, how many apples would Tommy have if he picked them up first? Earnie sharpened his pencil and scribbled the problem from the board into his notebook. He figured out the answer even before the first student raised her hand with the answer. Earnie peeked slightly to his left. Oh, it was Carla, his number one competitor in the math world. They had a secret friendly rivalry between them: to see who was the math blaster champion of the world. Or at least at PS 40.

Last year the school held a contest called the Big Math Challenge. Earnie and Carla tied for first place. It wasn't going to happen again. Not if Earnie could help it. This year the stakes were a pair of in-line skates, complete with protective gear. Caramel may have been better than Earnie in the other subjects, but math and current events belonged to him and him alone. Oh, yes, the in-line skates would be his!

Carla waved her hand as if it would fall off if the teacher didn't call her. Mrs. Collins nodded to her and the girl breathed out in relief. "The answer is two. Because Tommy's a gentleman, he would give Jane her apples back."

Earnie laughed and raised his hand. Mrs. Collins, who encouraged friendly competition between students, nodded for Earnie to give his answer.

"That's wrong, wra-ONG! Anybody knows that possession is nine tenths of the law. Tommy would own all of the apples legally if he picked them up first. And, if he was smart, he'd sell them back to Jane."

He finished his speech and tossed a smug smile towards his numerological foe. Carla rolled her eyes and didn't pay Earnie dirt.

Mrs. Collins was amazed. She thought both swers through and rendered her verdict.

"Since both of you are, in effect, correct, cause each situation could actually happen, vill give you both five points. Especially for tstanding creativity."

Earnie frowned. "Another tie? I'll never get ɔse skates if this keeps up."

Caramel chuckled, "Looks like the war of the ₌mber twins continues."

Suddenly, the janitor's voiced sprang through ₌ tiny speaker in Earnie's ear. He signaled to ₌ramel. The janitor was in the elevator talking to ₌eacher, Mr. Holland, who was on his way to the rking garage.

"Hey, Earl, how's it going?" asked Mr. ɔlland. "Say, could you let me borrow your nper cables? My car won't start again."

"Sure thing as a phone ring," said Earl. "Just me get this trash can to the Science Lab. I'll run wn and grab my jumper cables from my truck."

"You're the man, Earl. You're the man. I'll ₌et you by my car in ten minutes."

"All right, then."

Earnie looked at the clock on the wall. Their ₌ss wouldn't be over for seventeen more minutes.

"Kid, once the bell rings, we're only gonna have three minutes. That's one minute to get upstairs, one to look for the fang, and one to get to our next class."

"Hmm, then I guess we better run like the wind," said Caramel.

As Caramel watched the clock, he began to transfer energy from his body into his legs and feet. It was cheetah speed time.

The countdown began. 5...4...3...2...1...

RIIIIIIIIINNNNNNNNNNNNGGGGGGGGG!!!!!!!

Chapter Four:
Race for the Bone Medal

They raced downstairs and into the Science Lab. Earnie kept his eyes peeled on his digital stopwatch while Caramel scanned the room.

"So far nothing looks fishy, Earn. How are we doing on time?" Caramel asked, his eyes looking everywhere for the trash can of doom. His mind was on the fang. He hoped Earl hadn't dumped the trash.

"T-minus two minutes, thirty-one seconds and counting."

"I'm going to check the lab equipment closets." Caramel pulled open the double doors and found the can! There was no time to lose. He spotted a pair of yellow plastic work gloves, slipped them on, and dove into the trash. He tossed aside a variety of objects from discarded paper towels, notebook paper, coffee cups, to something, well...

"Earnie, come here, quick!"

"You found the fang?" Earnie looked into the can and gasped. The bottom of the can was covered with newspapers and litter. The fang stuck up from the litter. Next to it, in a neat stack, were the yellow bones of a small animal.

"Looks like a rabbit or a gerbil, maybe. Let's put them in a baggie so I can study them."

"Good idea, Earn." Caramel scooped up the fang and bones and dropped them into the two see-thru baggies his partner held open.

"Kid, wait."

"What is it?"

Earnie lifted the baggie to his eyes "See...there...there are some rough edges on the middle of a few of these bones. They look like...teeth marks!"

"Hmmm. I've got a bad feeling about this Earn. Follow me." Caramel and Earnie walked to the animal cages. There were three hamsters in one cage, a lizard in one, and the rabbit cage was empty. Caramel sighed.

"Looks like our meat-eating friend has moved onto live food. And Earl Ritter is suspect number one."

Chapter Five:
Teenagers Taste Great with
Bar-b-que Sauce

Several blocks away from Caramel's house, on Felder Street, a group of college students was having a moonlight bar-b-que. The table was set up in traditional picnic attire: checkerboard tablecloth, paper plates and cups, plastic utensils, the works. And on the grill was an assortment of food: spare ribs, chicken, and beef patties. There even were a few hot dogs thrown on the side for good measure. There was laughter, music and dancing. One of students pointed to the sky. The moon was full and had an erie yellow glow. Soon, all eyes were pointed straight up. The moon was so bright, even smoke from the grill couldn't block it out.

The students were having so much fun that no one noticed the shadow creeping up behind them. Slivers of moonlight reflected from it's eyes as the clouds opened away from the yellow disk in the night sky. The strange creature threw back it's head and howled once at the moon. Suddenly there was chaos as everyone screamed and bolted in different directions. Everyone was trying to get a good look at the thing but it moved like the night.

The creature dashed for the grill, after having scooped up every morsel of meat, cooked or raw. It howled again in satisfaction. The creature knocked over the table in search for more meat. All around it, students were running in circles. Some of the braver ones tried to attack the thing. But it howled and lashed threateningly with its claws. It ran after the students. Half an hour later, there was silence.

Chapter Six:
No Bones at the Dinner Table

At Earnie's house, the aroma of world famous dinner filled the air.

Mrs. Todd was busy putting the finishing touches on the steaks. She opened the lid of a pot and stirred string beans while checking on a side of sweet potatoes in the oven. Earnie's father carved the roasted chicken and placed some on each plate.

Caramel, Earnie and Kayin ate like there had been an announcement that no more food would be available the next day. It was Caramel's turn to eat at Earnie's house. Kayin had joined them for the first time since arriving in America. Kayin lived with a family down the block as a part of the exchange student program.

Kayin told stories of Scottish lore and, by popular request, tales of Scotland's most famous resident, the Loch Ness Monster!

"The monster, called Nessie by many people, is supposed to be a living dinosaur," Kayin said. He stuffed a huge fork-full of macaroni and cheese into his mouth.

"People have been coming to Scotland for

centuries trying to get a glimpse of her. But only a few have."

He tore off a chunk of steak that a full-grown man would have trouble with.

Kayin had requested his steak cooked rare. Caramel knew that rare meant almost raw. It was basically slightly browned on each side and served.

After Kayin scared the stuffing out of everyone, the table was cleared for a dessert tray prepared especially for the occasion.

Much to everyone's delight, dessert was cheesecake topped with cherries, apple turnovers, ice cream cake, and good ol' apple pie. Caramel was a strange eater; he liked cherries, but not on cheesecake. He scooped them off and made a neat pile on the side of the plate. It was the same when it came to raisins. He loved them out of the box but not in a danish. Earnie, on the other hand, ate anything. He'd eat cheesecake with a grasshopper in cherry sauce if you put it on a plate. Kayin was non-stop. He ate like he was the Loch Ness Monster's little brother.

Mr. Todd turned on the TV.

There was a picture of the moon and a guy in a straight jacket on the screen.

"What in the world?" Mr. Todd said as she turned the TV up.

The deep voice of the announcer said,

"And now, your channel seven Tanwood Evening News, with the award-winning Eye-Saw-t News Team, Kwame Stephens, Ira James and Kim Woods with weather...

"Good evening. Well, it's going to be a full moon tonight and Tanwood authorities are urging residents to stay inside. Through the ages, scientists have questioned the strange effect the full moon can have on people. And lately, here in Tanwood, things have been getting stranger and stranger. During the past five weeks, dozens of Tanwood pet owners have filed missing pet reports with the local authorities. And now animals are vanishing from schools as well as from the Tanwood Memorial Zoo. Here's what Police Commissioner Joanne Chow told our own Stella Shore..."

"There's nothing to be alarmed about, but we want people to be safe until we find the Raw Raider. We are hard at work to bring this case to a close. We have found animal bones but don't think they're related to this case."

"You heard it here first in our exclusive report. I'm Stella Shore for Tanwood News."

"Great chow, Mrs. Todd," Caramel said. He noisily slid his chair under the table. He was eager to get back on the trail of the so-called Raw Raider. He looked at both of Earnie's parents. "May we be excused to do some studying?"

"Sure, you boys give those books heck," Mr. Todd said. He laughed and reached for the newspaper. Mrs. Todd gave him a look.

"Thanks for a terrific meal, Mrs. Todd," Kayin added, arranging his dirty dishes into a neat stack. He pushed his chair away from the table and stood. He raced upstairs after Caramel and Earnie.

"Now you know I don't allow reading at my table, Howard." Said Mrs. Todd.

Her husband examined the table, grinning. "Hmmm. That's funny, I don't see your name anywhere on the table, sweetheart."

He pulled the paper to his face just in time to deflect a balled up paper towel. They both laughed and went into the livingroom to watch a little television.

Chapter Seven: On the Trail

Earnie's room was a combination hamper and bomb shelter. There were clothes, books, action figures, video games and pizza crusts everywhere. It was, in a word, frightening. But to Earnie it was home. To make up for the wreckage, there were some cool posters of aliens and space ships on the wall from his favorite show, the X Files. There were also some model kits that Earnie had built himself on shelves that shared space with various books on UFOs.

"Give me a second to clean up a little bit," Earnie said. He kicked similar objects into separate piles: pants, shirts, toys, food, etc., and called it a day. The room was now officially cleaned up.

"Big difference, Earn. Now I can see a part of the carpet," Caramel joked. He was amazed to find that it was green. Or was that mold? He managed to find a bean bag chair and plopped into it. Earnie dug into his backpack. Earlier in school, they had gone to the library for some research. Ms. Oswald had forgiven them for leaving such a mess. She helped them find the books they needed for their new case.

Earnie pulled the books on werewolves and

mythical monsters out and tossed a few to Caramel. Almost by second nature, Caramel dropped a piece of sugar free banana flavored bubble gum into his mouth. This little ritual helped him to think. He didn't have to ask whether his buddy wanted a piece. Earnie's open hand was in his face before he could peel a new stick from the package.

"Hey, Kayin, wants some gum? It's not raw like your steak, though."

"Sure, thanks." Kayin laughed. "You should try your steak that way. Tastes like you hunted the meat yourself."

Kayin reached for some of the books and plopped onto the floor.

Caramel flipped through the pages of a book on wolves. His eyes widened as they focused on one particular photo. Leaving his eyes glued to the page, he reached up and tapped Earnie's shoulder.

"Get a load of this, o' trusty sidekick."

"Wow! Look at those humongous fangs!"

"Exactly, and I think they come pretty close to the tooth we found at the school."

"Ye found a fang at the school today?" Asked Kayin, excited to be involved. "Lemme get a peek, boyos!"

"One fang comin' right up, hold the mayo!" Caramel stuck his foot through one of the handles of his own backpack and pulled it over. He extracted the tooth, which was enclosed in a plastic sandwich bag. He placed the real tooth on the book next to the photo.

"Kinda spooky, huh?"

Earnie and Kayin shook their heads. Earnie pressed the switch to turn on his computer. Then he grabbed a plastic ruler and a mini-cassette recorder.

"Here, let me measure the fang. I am the official research assistant, after all."

Caramel smiled. Earnie was unstoppable. He was going to help even if he had to jump into a volcano to do it. He passed him the plastic bag as Earnie started the recorder. *All great investigators read their findings aloud into a tape recorder*, Earnie thought.

"Earnie's log, sleuth-date one one seven point five. Hmm. This tooth, judging by the photo, is a canine incisor. It looks like it comes from a large dog or a wolf, but it's curved wrong somehow."

Earnie opened another book, as the computer's modem screeched and connected to the internet. The book was about human skeletons. He flipped until he reached a drawing of the jaw and teeth of an adult male.

"Aha! Some of the ridges on the fang resemble those found in human teeth, but I need to do a few more comparisons."

"I think it's keen how ye boys are detectives and such," said Kayin. Scotland's full of lore o' witches and werewolves. Can'na help ye with some o' tha' work?"

"Absolutely," Caramel said. "Never turn down new help, I always say. Pull up a chair...if you can find one without being bitten by a cobra. Look at this place!"

Caramel and Kayin sat at the computer. Earnie, lost in his books and tape recorder, remained on the floor-swamp.

"We're gonna do some research on the web, Earn'," said Caramel.

He typed the word 'werewolf' into the search engine and hit enter. The search resulted in a few references about fairy tales, one of them was Little Red Riding Hood.

"That was disappointing to say the least," Caramel muttered to himself.

He printed out the references that seemed interesting. Or ones that dealt with werewolf facts.

He knew there was another word for werewolves. He had heard it once or twice on a science fiction show on cable.

"Kayin, is there another word used in Scotland, to describe werewolves?"

"That's tha' only one I've heard. Sorry."

Caramel closed his eyes, activating his on-board brain computer.

"Computer, give me another word for werewolf." His brain computer responded,

"Searching...one moment please." After a few moments, the voice announced, "the word you are searching for is lyncanthrope!"

He opened his eyes and entered the word into the computer and again hit the enter key. This time he was rewarded with several pages and a few links to other spots of reference on the world wide web. He printed the index so he would be able to do further research later. He chewed faster on the gum. It helped him to absorb every detail, his eyes turning each word into pictures, so his brain could file them in their proper places.

"Kid, look at this." Earnie held up the book on human skeletons. The page depicted a close-up of the human jaw and its teeth. He held the tooth up next to the teeth on the page.

"According to this, this tooth is more human than animal, but humans don't have incisor teeth that are an inch or more in length."

Caramel nodded. "And according to this anthropology chart on the net, 95% of all werewolf reports are where people transform into wolves. Not the other way around. Which means Tanwood has a new neighbor...."

As if in stereo, the three boys uttered the word together..."Werewolf!"

Chapter Eight: Trouble at the Precinct

The soft amber glow of street lamps illuminated the newly redesigned Tanwood Police Department. There was a neat row of squad cars parked in front. Freshly trimmed hedges closely followed the outline of the building from front to back, with several openings which led to cobble stone walkways. All was well on the outside, but the inside was a different story.

Sgt. Mendez tried to calm down Mrs. Whitman. She was trembling terribly. He looked at his watch. It was nine p.m. And they had already filed forty reports from nervous citizens.

"Please, ma'am, try to relax. We'll make sure nothing happens to you." He helped her into a chair. "Look, can I get you some water? Coffee, maybe?"

Mrs. Whitman was Tanwood Church's lead choir singer.

"Thank you, officer, but it was horrible!" She wiped the tears from her eyes. "I still don't know whether or not I just imagined the whole thing."

"Just take your time and we'll figure this thing out, Mrs. Whitman."

He sat as his desk and adjusted the angle of his computer monitor.

"OK, ma'am, just start at the beginning and let's see what we can do here."

She hesitated for a moment, as if searching her memories for pieces to a jumbled puzzle. She sipped the coffee and closed her eyes. She exhaled deeply and opened her eyes again.

"I think I'm ready now. I-I was walking to my car from the supermarket on Spain Street. I noticed that the air was a little cooler than usual, and the moon was incredibly bright. There was a misty cloud around it. Very creepy! Well, I was just about to put my car keys into the door when I felt the hairs on my neck stiffen up, like a warning or something. But before I could turn around, this big, hairy creature knocked me to the ground and snatched one of my shopping bags," said Mrs. Whitman

"Hairy creature? Like a big dog or something?"

"More like those things in the movies. A... a werewolf!"

The officer stopped typing.

"We heard the same kinda story from a pizza delivery boy. His bike was attacked. He suffered only minor cuts and he's home by now."

He flipped through the stack of reports on his desk.

"We also heard from a whole bunch of college kids earlier. Said they were chased around by some hairy monster," said Sgt. Mendez.

"See, officer. I knew it!"

"Ma'am. Would you mind if our police sketch artist drew your description of the creature?"

"Not at all, officer. If it'll help nab that hairy maniac!"

"Uh, fine. Now let me get a few more details from you first. Exactly what was in the bag the wolf-man took from you?"

"That's the strangest part about it, officer," said Mrs. Whitman. "All of the bags were full of food. But the creature went for the bag with the fresh meat in it."

Officer Mendez's nose wrinkled at the thought. "Ah...what happened next?"

"Well, um, it up and ran off into the night. It was almost like he was never there, but as you can see," she held up what remained of the brown paper food bag, "he was real all right." The bag was torn by what appeared to be teeth. At that moment another shaking citizen walked into the front door.

"Help, there's a monster on the loose in Tanwood!"

Sgt. Mendez closed his eyes and sighed. "It's going to be a l–oo–o–ng night," he whispered to himself.

Chapter Nine:
Contestant Number Two

The next day at school during homeroom, Kayin walked in late again. No one paid much attention and classes went on as usual. During most of the day, Caramel and Earnie exchanged new notes about their werewolf research. Before they knew it, the lunch bell rang and they made a mad dash for the chow line.

"Hey, Kayin, Earnie said, "Mind if we join you?"

Kayin smiled. "No, my friends, not at all. "How goes tha' wolf hunt, eh?"

"Still no concrete evidence, but it always shows up." Caramel smiled back and opened his lunch bag.

"Yuch, tuna and peanut butter. Where'd my mother get that combination from?"

Kayin was eating a roast beef sandwich. It looked very undercooked to Caramel. As a matter of fact, the meat was mostly red and pink, with just a tiny amount of brown on the edges. But Kayin tore into the sandwich and was finished in two bites.

"Kayin, slow down, man. You hardly swallowed that," Caramel said, still deciding whether to be shocked or impressed.

"Yeah, you're supposed to inhale oxygen, not beef," Earnie added. He took a big gulp from his glass of milk, which left a bubbly mustache on his top lip.

The bell rang and it was back to the real world. Kayin's next class was English so he said good-bye and headed off. Caramel pulled Earnie to a corner.

"Tell me you noticed what I did, Earn'."

Earnie's face was a chalk board waiting to be written on.

"The beef, Earnie...the roast beef Kayin was eating. It was almost raw!"

Earnie's eyes widened and his jaw dropped. "No way...you don't think?"

"Earnie, Kayin is werewolf suspect number two!"

Chapter Ten:
Look, Ma, Fangs!

It was once again dinner time at the Park's residence. Ernie and Kayin were invited to join Kid and his family. They both sat politely at the table.

Caramel's mother had made her world famous liver, gravy, onions, and brown rice. Most of the kids at his school thought he was crazy for liking liver, but Caramel didn't care. He listened to his stomach, and rarely was it wrong (except for the time he ate two entire sweet potato and marshmallow pies. His stomach had been extremely wrong).

Many of Caramel's cases were approved by his parents because Sergeant Hutchinson agreed to chaperone him and Earnie. They weren't too thrilled with the idea of their son going to minor crime scenes. But Sergeant Hutchinson always stayed in the background, keeping his eyes on the boys at all times. And, most of the time, even Kid Caramel and Earnie weren't aware they were being followed by the watchful police guardian.

"So, how's your case coming, honey?" asked Mrs. Parks.

She served her growing son a man-sized portion. If

he couldn't eat it all now, there was always a second chance at lunch tomorrow. She might even throw a little peanut butter in there somewhere.

Waiting until everyone was served before attacking his plate, Caramel folded his arms and leaned his chair back on two legs. One quick look from his father told him that leaning in the chair was a bad idea. He straightened up to answer his mother.

"So far, the case is coming along just fine, but there is one teeny problem."

"What's wrong, son?" asked his father.

"Uh, Earnie and I found something that may turn the whole thing upside-down. We think the crimes are being committed by...a werewolf."

Both of his parents remained silent and looked at each other.

"Caramel, I think you and Earnie might be taking your detective business in the wrong direction. You two should stay away from nonsense and research actual cases, if anything," said his father.

"I have to agree with your father on this one, Caramel. Monsters aren't real. I'd rather you stick to real cases myself."

Caramel shook his head slowly in disappointment.

"I knew you wouldn't believe me, but I thought I'd tell you about it anyway."

"OK, I'll entertain the conclusion you and Earnie have reached," said his father, skeptically. "What evidence do you have to prove that there's a werewolf running amuck in Tanwood?"

"It's kinda disgusting but can I show it to you anyway?" Caramel asked.

His mother squinted her eyes.

"How disgusting are we talking about? I mean, we're still eating dinner, son."

Caramel smiled. "Oh, it's not that bad. I'll be right back. It's upstairs in my backpack."

In a screech of sneaker rubber against the floor, he dashed across the kitchen and up the stairs. Using the speed of the wind, Caramel was back in the kitchen before anyone could blink. "We have two baggies worth of clues right here."

Earnie stood and took one of the baggies from his partner. He held it up so the light would shine through. "Ta daaa!"

Mrs. Parks gasped. "Why'd you boys bring animal bones in my house?"

"Because this rabbit was a meal to our werewolf," said Earnie, nodding to Caramel. Caramel held up his baggie.

"You see, mom, this tooth matches the bite on this rabbit's leg. My science teacher matched bacteria from the tooth to our little bony friend.

Caramel's father suddenly shushed everyone. "The news is on. It's a special report."

Tanwood News Special Report

"This is Kwame Stephens live at a press conference at City Hall. The mayor is away on vacation but we are being briefed by Police Commissioner Joanne Chow. She's coming to the microphone now."

"Quiet, please. As you may have heard, there is some kind of large animal loose in our vicinity. Police have received many eyewitness reports and have captured a large stray dog this evening." A house filled the TV screen. "We believe the animal was coming and going from this house, owned by a Mr. Earl Ritter, janitor at PS 40. Police teams are investigating the area but there has been no sign of Mr. Ritter at this time."

"We will keep you posted as events develop. And we'll have a full report at ten. I'm Kwame Stephens for Tanwood News."

Caramel, Earnie and Kayin by turn, all looked at the adults. I-told-you-so was written all over their faces.

"May we go to Earl Ritter's house with Sergeant Hutchinson?" Caramel asked with a grin. "The police caught a dog. The werewolf is still out there."

His father sighed heavily. "I don't see why not."

"But we want you back in this house by nine-thirty, understood?" his mother added.

Jacket sleeves were on their way up each boy's arm before she could take another breath. They all mumbled "yes" as they headed to the phone. Caramel dialed the precinct.

"Sergeant Hutchinson, please. Yes, tell him it's Kid Caramel. Sure, I'll hold."

"Kid Caramel. Long time no see," said the sergeant. "What can Tanwood's Finest do for you tonight?"

"I hear you guys caught a stray dog. But my friend Earnie and Kayin would like to visit Earl Ritter's house."

"You think there's still trouble, don't you, Caramel?" asked the sergeant.

"You know me well, sir," Caramel laughed. "Would you mind sending a squad car for us?"

"You want free sodas and chips with that?" Sergeant Hutchinson joked. "I'll meet you boys at the house in half an hour. And expect the car in fifteen minutes. Officer Kim's in your neck of the woods."

"See you soon and thanks." Caramel hung up the phone and thundered up the stairs.

Earnie started packing their special equipment, and filled a bookbag full of backup supplies for Kayin. Fifteen minutes later, a squad car beeped its horn and the boys piled in like it was a blue-and-white taxi cab. Officer Kim told them what he knew about the animal that was caught. It was a larger-than-normal German Shepherd whose family lost him at a park. Caramel didn't like the way it sounded but soon, they'd know the truth.

The house was just around the corner. Officer Kim dropped the boys off and said he'd return with Sergeant Hutchinson in ten minutes. He said if they needed anything, officers were questioning Earl's neighbors and would be back every few minutes.

Earl's house was in a surprisingly bad state of disrepair for a place owned by a janitor. There were planks of siding that would fall off from the slightest gust of wind. The paint was chipped on the columns that supported the second floor patio porch. The lawn hadn't been cut since the fall of Rome. Caramel double checked the address. The police had to have made a mistake. The house looked like it came straight out of a theme park. Kid Caramel switched his senses to bio-scan so he could detect life signs. He noticed two officers a few houses down. As far as he could tell, there were animals like birds and squirrels, cats and dogs at almost every house on the block. Except this one.

Caramel, Earnie and Kayin entered the house as quietly as they could. Caramel switched to Ninja-mode and readied his hands for immediate bad-guy-bashing action. It was just after eight o'clock and it was getting chillier. Kid Caramel could smell the staleness in the air. Thick screens of dust were everywhere. He could see the moonlight reflecting off the silken spider webs in the corners. The young detective became one with the shadows, one with the night. They would be his allies. Kid Caramel knew his mission: to gather evidence, not to engage the enemy. At least not yet, not now.

With the stealth of a cat, Caramel Parks inched across the living room to what looked like a trunk of some kind. A noise caught his attention and he reached into his vest. He removed a handful of aluminum foil throwing stars. They were called *shuriken* by real Japanese Ninja.

Caramel breathed in relief. Kayin and Earnie held their breath in. It was only a mouse that skittered from its hiding place into a small hole in the floor. Once again, another enemy was spared a most painful fate. He placed the *shuriken* into his vest and continued on to the trunk.

"Hoo, hoo," Caramel signaled to Earnie by mimicking an owl. It was another classic Ninja trick. In a moment, his partner was at his side. Caramel held up three fingers, indicating, in codes they always practiced, that he needed the flashlight. Like a nurse, Earnie slapped it into Caramel's waiting hand. The lens of the flashlight was covered with a blue supermarket grocery bag. This made the light less harsh and kept them in the shadows for ultra-stealth ability.

Kayin grabbed another bag-covered flashlight and vanished around a corner.

"I'll check tha' next room."

Caramel whispered for him to come back but Kayin's footsteps grew softer and softer. A door creaked open in the distance then slowly creaked shut again.

"What do we do now?" asked Earnie in a whisper.

Caramel shrugged his shoulders and pointed the light around the room. Then he pointed down.

"We open the trunk." Caramel signaled to Earnie again. They both took out staplers from their bags.

"Remember what our research told us about werewolves. They can be hurt or cured by silver. So be ready to use the silver staples if we have to."

They opened the lid and the room filled up with the smell of a zoo. Caramel and Earnie nodded to each other and covered their mouths and noses with the bottoms of their ninja masks. Caramel aimed the blue flashlight beam into the trunk. There were dozens of pet collars inside, but thank goodness, no bones. And it only smelled like fur and not rotting meat.

Now there were two mission objectives: to find and stop the werewolf; and to rescue and return dozens of missing pets to their rightful homes.

"Earnie, write down the names of the pets from these collars while I search the next room."

His partner nodded and took out a pen and pad.

Before Earnie could put pen to paper, a scream echoed through the house.

"Kid, that sounded like Kayin!"

"Kayin, are you OK?" yelled Caramel. There was no answer as they ran in the direction of the scream. "Kayin! Earl must've got him, Earnie! Earl must be the werewolf!"

A spine chilling howl ripped through the dark night, stopping both boys in their tracks.

"ARRROOOOOOWWRRRRRGGGHHHHHHH!!!!!"

Neither of them had ever heard anything so scary. To Caramel, it sounded like it came from something that was part wolf, part lion, part tyrannosaur, and part gym teacher. Both boys instantly bolted up the stairs to the third floor as another terrifying howl shook the house.

"AWWOOOOOOOOOOOOORRRRRRGGGHHHHHH!!!!"

Caramel's owl-sight kicked in. He could tell there were exactly fourteen steps left to climb. He and Earnie rushed into the first available room and closed the door as quietly as possible. Caramel summoned the strength of the elephant spirits. He pushed a dresser in front of the door.

They looked around the room. It was full of cooking supplies: flour, oil, sugar, yeast, and large foil pans. The room must have been once used as an upstairs kitchen.

Downstairs, the creature paused, sniffed the air carefully to catch the scent of the boys, and began to climb. THUD THUMP THUD. It let out another

"H⊙⊙⊙⊙⊙⊙⊙⊙WWWWWWWWLLLLLLLL!!!!!"

and swung up an arm with such force that it knocked loose a part of the banister. The wooden beam spiraled down the stairs and crashed far below. Using it's enhanced sense of sight, the werewolf scanned the stairs, picking up heat signatures from the boys' hands on the banister. He could see their fingerprints on the railing and the heat left behind by the friction of their sneakers on each step.

Ahhh...the footprints go to the left...and into...that room, the creature thought aloud in a deep, scratchy voice. The creature growled a sinister laugh and proceeded upward.

"Kid, what are we gonna do? That-that thing's coming to get us!"

"This I know, Earn. Now give me a second to think about this."

There was a phone on a wooden table in the corner. "Earnie, call 911. Also, get the micro cassette recorder going. We need to tape one of those howls if anyone's gonna believe us."

Caramel closed his eyes and looked into his Emergency Brain Computer. There were gears turning in one section, and a computer-like control board in the other. And both were working at full power. He walked to the control panel in his brain marked 'Danger: And how to get out of it'. "Computer, I need to know the best ways to escape from a werewolf."

His brain computer replied, "Working. One moment please."

"What do you mean 'one moment?' Me and Earnie will be ground beef in one moment. Hurry up!"

The brain computer reported in. "I suggest the two of you try to climb out of the window and down the trees. Then you can run to safety."

"Thanks, gotta go-"

"Wait, I'm not finished yet," the brain computer said.

Caramel suddenly heard the door to the room make a cracking sound. The werewolf was kicking and clawing at it. The sound of its claws on the wood made his teeth ache. He returned his attention to his brain. "Any day now, brain!"

"Cover the floor with oil from the baking supplies."

"Great idea, brain. See ya soon. I hope." Caramel switched off the Emergency Brain Computer. He snapped back into his body and turned to Earnie.

"Let's both grab a few of those bottles of cooking oil and coat the floor with it. We'll work our way from the door and climb out the window."

"Gotcha," Earnie said.

In a few seconds, the floor was soaked in oil. The boy ninjas climbed out of the window and onto the ledge. Just then the door to the room gave way to the werewolf's fierce pounding. It scanned the room for its prey, infrared vision hunting for heat traces.

But the wolf-man didn't have to search long, because he heard dry twigs snapping. The tell-tale sound was coming from...outside of the window. In a mad dash, the creature lunged forward but slipped uncontrollably towards the window at full speed! Trying desperately to slow himself down, the werewolf crashed head-first into the window, shattering the glass in a million tiny shards. The impact shook the room and bags of flour rained down, bursting all over the creature's body.

The creature heard voices coming from outside

"Hey, fur-face, we're down here!"

"Yeah, fleabag!"

Angrily, it struggled to it's feet and climbed out of the window. It breathed heavily as it reached for the nearest tree branch. The monster carefully worked it's way to the thick trunk and grabbed it with both paws. Or, at least, tried to grab it. The trunk too was covered in oil, and before the werewolf could recover from it's mistake, it found itself sliding down at full speed toward the ground.

SLAAMMM!!!

As soon as the monster hit the ground, Caramel ran at it and put a silver staple in it's leg. It barely howled out, so great was the other pain it was dealing with.

The clouds peeled away from the moon and the light reached through the branches and brushed the leaf-covered ground.

"Do you think it's...you know?" asked Earnie. He was hiding behind a tree.

"No, he's not dead. I think he's breathing, Earn." Caramel looked at the werewolf then at the stapler. "Doesn't look like he's changing back to human..."

As the clouds swirled around the ever-brightening moon, another werewolf leapt from around the corner of the house!

"RAAAAARRRRRRRRHHHHH!"

"Earnie...this can't be happening!"

Earnie crept around the tree trunk for cover. His mouth fell open. "AAAHHHH!"

The werewolf on the ground sprang up, holding his chest. It backed up along the side of the house. He was pointing at the second werewolf.

"Keep it away from me!" the creature shouted. The second werewolf closed in.

"Earnie, round two on the staple guns!" ordered Kid Caramel.

"Which one do we staple, Kid? Which one?" Earnie asked in a panic. One werewolf was bad enough, but two?

"We better pick one and team up on it."

"I pick the one who can talk. Maybe that first staple helped to bring him back. He needs a little more silver in him!" Earnie yelled.

"Now that's a logical idea. Let's do it!'

As the boys ran at the talking werewolf, it waved its hands at them.

"Noooo! No more staples!" The creature put its hands to its head an lifted it off! A man's face looked them in the eye. "Those things hurt, as sure as Bert!"

"Earl?" both boys said together.

Suddenly Caramel remembered the other werewolf and spun around. It wasn't attacking. As a matter of fact, it was...laughing!

The other werewolf took his mask off too. "Aye, my friends. 'Tis me, Kayin McIntyre at your service."

"Wow! You really scared me pretty good," said Earnie.

"Aye. That was Kid's plan, Earnie."

"You see, Earn', I couldn't tell you what we were gonna do," Caramel said. "We had to make sure you were as scared as Earl. Or he would never have believed Kayin was a real werewolf. And he would never have taken his mask off."

"We figured two could play at werewolf actin'," said Kayin with a grin. "We borrowed some money from my exchange brother. Then we rented this costume."

"Great job, boyo," replied Caramel.

Just then, police sirens wailed in from the distance and grew closer.

Cars screeched in front of the house and footsteps surrounded the house. Doors inside the house slammed and banged and then other footsteps headed to the backyard.

Sergeant Hutchinson pointed his flashlight in the boys' faces. "Caramel...Earnie? Are you boys all right?" He looked at the third boy? "Let me guess, you must be Kayin."

"Yes, sir," Kayin nodded.

Hutchinson looked at Kayin.

"In America one week and these guys have you dressing up like a bear." he said, laughing. Sergeant Hutchinson noticed another person in a bear outfit. "And who might that be?"

"That's Earl Ritter," Caramel answered. "He's the one who's been stealing pets and taking all that meat."

"What's your get up, Earl?" Asked Sergeant Hutchinson. He pulled Earl's arms behind his back and handcuffed him. He read him his rights and asked him why again.

"I was stealing all those pets, sure as bets all right," said Earl, slow drawl in full effect. "I was feeding them animals real good like to get 'em fat. Then I was gonna sell 'em to a scientifical like lab for lots of money. That way I could quit my job and live in the lap of luxury, like huckleberry."

"That one didn't rhyme, Mr. Ritter," said Caramel. "So, where are the pets?"

"In the basement. I ain't hurt none of 'em," said Earl.

"Well, I'm putting you in the lap of the jail system, Earl. Let's go." The sergeant said.

"All right then," said Earl.

Everyone jumped as a long sound filled the air.

"H☺☺☺☺☺☺☺☺WWWWWWWWLLLLLLLLL!!!!!"

They all spun around, Earl included.

"Whoops, sorry about that," said Earnie. He had pressed the play button on the mini recorder by bumping into the tree.

The boys laughed as Earl was escorted away. The janitor would have a lot of explaining to do.

"So, who's up for some video games?" Caramel asked.

Up above, the moon was as full as ever. There were no monsters on the loose. And all was quiet and just fine tonight in Tanwood.

The End

Visit Kid Caramel and his friend on the web!
Just go to:
www.diehardstudio.com
and e-mail us at diehardhq@earthlink.net

For other great Just Us Books stuff go to:
www.justusbooks.com

Coming in *Kid Caramel #3:*
Mess at Loch Ness

Someone has finally discovered the Loch Ness Monster but her secret is going to remain just that, a secret. As soon as she's discovered she's stolen! Can Kid Caramel, Earnie and their new pal Kayin rescue Nessie while solving the mystery of the ghost of Urquhart Castle? Don't miss it!

Tell us what you think about
Kid Caramel's *second adventure!*

Name _____

Address _____

City_____ State _____ Zip_____

Birthdate_____ Grade _____

Teacher's Name _____

Who is your favorite character in this book? Do you know of
anyone with a personality like Caramel? Or Earnie?_____

_____

Write down the title of this book.

_____

What topics would you like to see treated in future
KID CARAMEL™ books?_____

_____

How did you get your first copy of KID CARAMEL™?
   ❏ Parent?   ❏ Gift?   ❏ Teacher?   ❏ Library?   ❏ Other?
Are you looking forward to the next title in this series?
Why or why not? _____

_____

_____

Any other comments? _____

_____

Send your reply to:
KID CARAMEL™   c/o Just Us Books, Inc.
356 Glenwood Avenue, East Orange, NJ 07017
or email to: justusbook@aol.com

To our readers:

Hey there! This is from Dwayne, the guy who wrote this tale of action and mystery. Once again I hope you enjoyed this action-packed romp in the exciting world of Kid Caramel, Private Investigator. For those of you who really love mysteries, there will be a cool Mystery of the Month on the web! (Address below). Each month, you could win cool stuff from Just Us Books if you're one of the first five kids to solve it! You can also send letters to me about the series or you can write to Kid Caramel himself. He'll even write you back! We look forward to hearing from each and every one of you soon. We've got plenty of prizes to give away so visit us at **www.diehardstudio.com** and at **www.justusbooks.com**

Peace,

Dwayne J. Ferguson
Being cool is just being you